From Burglar to Football Star

Books FOR Boys

IAN WHYBROW
ILLUSTRATED BY MARK BEECH

Hodder
Children's
Books

For Dav... ...rs, past and present, at ...er United F.C.

Up to No Good

My mum and dad used to have to work all hours. OK, I had my big sister Chrissie looking after me, cooking my meals. But I was upset.

It annoyed me that they were never there for me like other parents. They never dropped me off at school or gave me big worried hugs like other kids used to get. How could they? Mum was a nurse and Dad did painting and decorating. They were gone before I was awake.

Anyway, I started acting up, getting moany, being awkward. I didn't like this, wouldn't do that. Next thing I know there's a new telly in my room, a big one.

Aha! I thought.

They're feeling guilty. They know they're not treating me properly. Right, then, they've asked for it.

Stupid, I know, but I felt I deserved to have more nice things to make up for not getting enough attention.

So I started thieving.

A Brush with PC Beetroot

Jimmy Skinner is my name and, yeah,
I am small and skinny, compared to
my sister Chrissie. She's the strongest
girl I know. She does a lot of what
they call "pumping iron" and
she's well good at all
games, 'specially
soccer. There's
nothing she can't
do with a football.
She had a trial with

Arsenal Ladies when she was fourteen but Dad wasn't having any of it. He told her sorry but he and mum needed her to be home to keep an eye on me. Our estate can be a bit rough, see.

She never actually said anything about me holding her back, but sometimes, like if I was playing up, she would give me *The Look*. That was it. Back off. If you get *The Look*, just roll over. You don't want to cross Chrissie.

The thing about being built like me is, people don't notice you. So they don't have the faintest idea that you're quietly sneaking off with their property. And if you're fast – like I've always been – it doesn't matter if they *do* notice. Because how are they ever going to catch you?

The Artful Dodger – that was me, king of the sweet-swervers. All you had to do was hang about at the back of a sweet shop while the owner was busy serving lots of other kids. Then bingo! a chocolate bar might just happen to jump into your pocket. Or some chewing gum. And I would say to myself: *They've got piles of this stuff. They're never going to miss a couple of little things. Anyway, I deserve them.*

Stealing was thrilling and it made me feel smart. I kidded myself that the people I was robbing were stupid for letting me get away with it.

It was ages before anybody had a clue that I was on the take. Trust Lightbulb to be the first one to catch me. He's this big flashy kid with mad hair, runs around with Raven and Dippy Woodgate. They were all older and bigger than me but Lightbulb was the boss. He was the oldest, the biggest, the hardest; and he knew things. He was a wicked spitter.

Round our neighbourhood, you could run into the Lightbulb mob most days if you weren't careful. They were always hanging around together in the playground with the busted swings. Mostly they liked to

chase other kids off the roundabout
and kick themselves round in slow
circles, talking secrets. They were a
nasty bunch, 'specially Dippy
Woodgate. He would punch your
head as soon as look at you.

Still, I guess you could say I was
drawn to them. I liked the way they
dressed, the way they looked, all
free and confident. And there I
was, mostly on my own feeling
sorry for myself.

Anyway, there I was, just stepping towards the door of the mini-mart with a pocketful of pick-and-mix that I'd just nicked. Suddenly a deep voice made me jump: "Oy, you!"

Straight away, the shop-keeper looked my way. I froze and felt the blood drain out of me. But he wasn't the one who'd shouted. It was Lightbulb. He was charging down one aisle towards me. Raven and Dippy cut me off in the other aisle and rammed me like bumper cars. "Naughty boy, Skinny!" they yelled and they shoved me outside into the street.

"Pack it in, you lot!" called the shopkeeper. "Behave yourselves!"

And then he carried on serving the kid at the front of the queue.

Once we were outside, Lightbulb pinned my arms behind my back while the others dipped into my pockets and grabbed my loot. And my mobile. "Oo! What we got here?" teased Raven, popping a toffee into his gob and sharing out the rest with his mates.

"Quick! Call the coppers!" yelled Dippy Woodgate, loud enough for everyone on the shop to hear, including the shopkeeper. "He's been robbin' ya!"

"P-please …" I stammered. "Keep your voice down!"

"A right little tea-leaf, aintcha Skinny?" said Lightbulb with an ugly laugh. "But don't worry. We won't tell your mummy. Not if you do as you're told."

"Look out!" hissed Dippy. "It's PC Beetroot! Leg it!" He gave me a shove that sent me flying and dumped me on to my backside. They were off round the corner before I could even get to my feet, so I was the only one the red-faced policeman on the bike got a proper look at. He started pedalling like mad towards me.

At the same time, the shop keeper came flying out of his door. "Hey! I'm sick of kids coming in here stealing my stuff!" he growled

and made a grab
at me.

I snatched my arm
away and I was off
like the wind.

"Stop him! He's a
shoplifter!" he
yelled.

"Hold it!" warned the
copper as I got into my stride and
cut down an alley. "Wait! I want a
word with you!"

I didn't feel like a chat so
shinned up on to a high wall,
pausing only to knock over a
couple of empty wheelie bins to
block his way while I put on a spurt
along my brick tightrope.

"I've had a good look at you,

sunshine!" bellowed PC Beetroot, dismounting and calmly picking up the bins. "And I never forget a face! Sooner or later we're going to meet each other again. And then I'll have you! You hear me?"

I Become a Squeezer

For the next couple of days I was
worried sick. Then one late afternoon,
it came: the knock at the door. I let
Chrissie answer it. "What do you
want?" I heard her say with more than
a hint of warning in her voice.

"Sorry to disturb you, like," came
a low voice, not the policeman's
but Lightbulb's. It was weird hearing
him being polite. "But my mate
Raven found this mobile in the street.

We think it might belong to your brother."

"Jimmy!" called Chrissie. "Lightbulb Lewis wants to talk to you." She swept back to the kitchen. I passed her in the hall. She gave me *The Look*. "And don't you be long," she warned. "The beans are nearly ready."

I knew the gang had taken my mobile out of my pocket when they took the sweets off me. I hadn't expected to get it back.

"Hello, James," said Lightbulb as I pulled the front door closed to keep our conversation private from Chrissie. He held out the phone. "Here you go."

I took it, not sure what was going on. "We're in the same game, you and us," said Lightbulb, sounding a bit too casual. "And you're pretty good." I knew they were into housebreaking, which wasn't the same game as shoplifting at all, but I knew better than to say anything.

"We like you," said Dippy.

"Cause you're quick, see? You can climb and all. And you're a lot smaller'n us," said Raven, mussing my hair.

"Which is why you're going to be our Squeezer," said Lightbulb.

"You what!" I exclaimed. "A Squeezer? Me? You're kidding!"

"You ain't got no choice, mate," said Dippy, knuckling the side of my head. "Meet us outside the Coffee Cake at eleven o'clock or we drop a note into the police station and let PC Beetroot know where you live."

Gulp!!! I gulped. "Eleven o'clock at *night?*" I said. "My mum and dad'll be home then! How can I?"

"You're cunning, you are," said Raven, showing his teeth. "You'll think of a way."

"Now go and eat your tea like a good boy," Lightbulb teased. "And go careful. Nobody likes spilled beans, do they?"

Trapped

I was all mixed up. Part of me just wanted to keep my head down, but another part of me was really excited. I knew that gangs of burglars depend on Squeezers to get them into locked houses. Here was my chance to show the Lightbulb Boys that I had guts, and earn some respect.

Mum and Dad both had a peep through my bedroom door when they got in but I did my best imitation of

Sleeping Beauty for them and they crept away. Good thing they never looked under the duvet or they'd have seen I had my tracksuit on.

By ten to eleven they were showered and into bed. I gave them five minutes to get their heads down and then hoped for the best. I was out of my window and down the drainpipe in seconds flat, so I made it to the Coffee Cake by five past eleven.

"You're late," Dippy Woodgate said, appearing out of the shadow of the doorway and giving me a shove.

"Leave him," ordered Lightbulb, stepping out with Raven from another dark place. He turned up his collar and gave his mad hair a shake. "This way."

We hurried after him along the deserted High Street. It felt weird being out there in the spooky orange light and my heart was banging away like mad. "Wait!" hissed Lightbulb, suddenly ducking into the service road next to the sports shop.

"What's up?" whispered Raven as we pressed our backs to the wall.

"Thought I heard somebody following us," Lightbulb whispered back. He risked a sneaky look round the corner. "No … we're OK. Let's go."

The house we were going to rob was in Maple Avenue, they told me. It turned out to be one of those big old-fashioned ones with a row of windows built into the roof for an extra room in the attic. One of them was open – just a crack.

"The owners are on holiday," said Raven with a grin as we scuttled round to the back.

"No alarm, but she's locked up tight, except for up there," murmured Lightbulb.

"W-what? There's no way I'm climbing up there ..." I protested.

"You div!" sneered Raven. "*Nobody* could climb up there. You're goin' in round the back."

It was a lot darker in the back garden but there was enough moonlight to see the little frosted bathroom window on the first floor. "Off you go," said Lightbulb, staring upwards and shaking the creeper that was clinging to the back wall. "This should hold your weight. Get in the window, come downstairs, unlock the back door and we'll do the rest."

Boy, I was quick! I was up that
creeper like a monkey and through
the top toilet window like greased
lightning. I put my head out on
to the landing, ready to hurry
downstairs. That was when I got the
shock of my life. A car screeched to
a halt in the avenue. Everything
inside the house was suddenly lit
up by a ghostly blue flashing light.

"It's the coppers! Run for it!" I heard Raven croak. After that I heard doors slam, whistles, shouts, footsteps running on gravel.

"They're getting away across the back gardens!" came a booming policeman's voice.

A short while later, two other people burst through the front door and snapped the lights on. I couldn't move. A rabbit in the headlights; that was me.

Somebody ran to the back door.

"The back door's still bolted. No way they could have got in through here," came a woman's voice.

"Right, Mrs Jenkins," answered a man's voice from by the front door. "Well there's no sign of a forced entry through the front. So thanks to your quick thinking and dialling 999, the property's safe. Gosh, your neighbour will be pleased they left the keys with you! I reckon we managed to scare the intruders away before they even got into the house. Still, just to be on the safe side, I'll have a look around upstairs for you."

"They've got me. I'm dead," I thought as the stairs began to creak.

And before I could move a muscle, a strong hand got hold of my collar and lifted me right off my feet.

Chrissie to the Rescue

I found myself being bundled into a dark room that was warm and cramped. I couldn't see a thing, but I felt like I was getting smothered in some sort of soft material. My mouth was held shut by the hand that had grabbed me even though I was too scared to struggle or shout.

It was ages before the hand let go. Bit by bit the door cracked open and some light leaked in. Finally a voice said, "That's it. They've gone. We can leave." I knew that voice! Flippin' 'eck – it was my sister!

"Don't ask," she said, as she steered me by the neck downstairs and – when she was sure the coast was clear – out through the front door.

On the way home, I found out bit by bit that she was the person Lightbulb had heard following us. She had smelt a rat when he had come knocking on our door and kept an extra-specially close eye on me.

So while we were creeping round the back of the house to break in, she had managed to clamber up the front of the house! Raven said it was impossible but he didn't know Chrissie. When she heard the police car coming, she crept down, pulled me into an airing cupboard and covered us both over in bath towels and blankets.

Sign Here . . . Or Else

What's going on? I kept saying to myself. Chrissie was taking being my minder seriously, but d'you know what? She never said a dicky-bird to Mum or Dad!

I came home from school the following afternoon and I found something waiting for me on my bed: shorts, T-shirt, socks, trainers. And a brand new football.

"Here's the deal," she said,

bouncing the football off my head. "This goes everywhere you go. And until I say different, everywhere you go, I go. You give up thieving. You steer clear of Lightbulb Lewis and his scummy mates. And you take your orders from me. Otherwise, you are REALLY on your own because I will NEVER speak to you again."

I opened my mouth but nothing came out. "Sign here," she said, holding out a piece of paper.

"What is it?"

"It says you're interested in something decent for a change," she said. "You're joining Lexley Youth FC."

The Hard Work Begins

Although I'd signed on the dotted line and said I'd like to try their facilities, I didn't get near Lexley for a month.

"Hey, where are you two off to?" said Dad. It was six o'clock the next morning. He was just taking Mum up her cup of tea and there were Chrissie and me in our running kit, each with a football under our arm.

"Training," said Chrissie.

Torture, more like.

We got to the Rec. She looked at her watch. "It's two kilometres round the outside. Stay close to the fence. We'll do it in eighteen minutes."

"Piece of cake," I muttered.

"Do what I do," Chrissie said sternly, dropping her ball on to the ground. Then she was off like a rocket, keeping the ball close, never letting it get more than a few centimetres in front of her. I thought I'd get away with a boot-and-chase, but no such luck. Every time she saw the ball get beyond my control she would shout "Stop! Ten press-ups!" or "Hold it! Fifteen sit-ups."

I thought I was fit, but it took

nearly 25 minutes to do that first circuit and by the time we'd got round, I was shattered. She let me pant for exactly one minute. "Again!" she barked. And we were off.

I lost count of the number of press-ups she made me do on the first few mornings, so it didn't take me all that long to make sure that football stuck like glue to my bootlaces.

When we arrived home after the first training-session, I rushed straight from the front door into the kitchen and threw open the fridge. "Out! I'm doing breakfast," she barked. "You stink. You need a shower."

"Charming," I said, but I went and had a shower. By the time I came downstairs again and sat at the table I was starving. "Where's my Chocksie Pops?" I demanded, seeing what Chrissie had put out for me.

"Forget that sugary rubbish. You're eating porridge and a fruit smoothie."

"I hate porridge and I hate

fruit!" I protested. "You can't make me eat this!"

But she could. All it took was *The Look*. "Remember our deal," she said. After that it was like it or lump it.

A week later, I did a couple of record-breaking circuits of the Rec, even overtaking Chrissie in the last ten metres. I waited for her to say *well done* or something. Instead, she grabbed my football and put it aside. "Right," she announced, pressing the button on her stop-watch, "you've got five minutes to get my ball off me. Otherwise, no telly tonight."

"What!" I said. My favourite programme was on and she knew it, so I tried a sliding tackle. Calmly, she flipped the ball over my body and stepped out of the way of my trailing leg.

"Red card," she said without raising her voice. "Four minutes forty-five seconds."

I got up and tried to bundle the ball out from between her feet. I went at her like a terrier but I never got near it. She simply brought her left leg round between me and the ball and rolled away from me with her right foot. I tried tapping her heels and tripping her up, but she was ready for that, too.

She stepped sideways, and then trod on my leading foot. Hard.

Ouch! I put my hands on my hips and sulked. "Work!" she said and tempted me to lunge at her again.

And again. And again – with no joy. "Time's up," she said.

After my shower, I went up to my room and found that Chrissie had taken my telly.

"I know my rights!" I yelled.

"I'm hanging on to your rights for the time being, Mister Squeezer," she said cheerfully from downstairs.

I found the book she had left on my bed. It was called *Top Tips to make your Season Special.*

"I'm not reading that," I mumbled, not wanting to risk her hearing me.

"I heard that," she called.

Seeing there wasn't much else to do that night, I read it anyway. It was quite good, actually. I could see where I was going wrong in the tackle. I was watching Chrissie making those fancy *this-way*, *that-way* moves with her upper body. And all the time I should have been watching the ball!

A Couple of Rookies

I remember that first Wednesday evening in the gym with the Lexley Youth lads. There was me and this other leggy kid wanting to join. Well … me not really wanting to and him dead keen.

"All right, Dave?" Chrissie said to the coach. "You've brought him, then, Christine," he said, smiling and shaking her hand. "Is he anywhere near as good as you?"

"He'll do," she said.

Dave shook my hand and told her to pick me up in an hour. "This is Dan Warner," he said, introducing me to the other kid who'd come for a try-out. When he smiled, he showed a wide mouthful of gappy teeth. He seemed too big for his shirt. "It's Dan's first time here, too," Dave told me. "Ready for a warm-up?"

"Not half!" said Dan, all keen. I said nothing. I wasn't sure if I really fancied this at all.

The regulars were out on the floor already, doing my ears in with the squeaks from their trainers.

It wasn't long before Dave was giving out red bibs for a five-a-side game, Reds v. Shirts, with me and Dan both playing for the Reds. Dan was put on the left wing and I was put out on the right. None of the other kids took any notice of me but they all took the rise out of Dan. "What's the weather like up there?" asked one joker.

I thought it took guts for Dan to keep smiling and get on with it the way he did, but you could see that the mickey-taking was putting him off. He was all arms and legs and clumsy great feet.

"Sorry … sorry!" he kept saying.

It didn't take me long to see that we had all those cocky Shirts kids beat. I had no trouble running rings round them and I had plenty of puff left when their lungs were bursting. In the final minutes Reds were up by five goals. Our goalie slipped the ball to me up close to our goal line. I sprinted off, left three Shirts standing and saw Dan lolloping towards their goal. He wasn't looking but he got

lucky. I dinked the ball and it bounced off the side of his head, right into the top corner.

"Nice going," Dave said afterwards just as Chrissie turned up to fetch me. "We'll see how you go on grass this Saturday. Are you OK for a trial with the Under-10s up at Norton School at ten o'clock?"

I nodded. It was nice to get some praise. He hadn't said anything to Dan, though, so I said, "How about Lofty? It was a good header, that last one of his."

Dave scratched his bald patch. He didn't seem too sure. Then he turned and saw how far Dan's head had dropped. "Oh, er, I don't see why not. Yeah. Always handy to

have a tall feller in the box," he said.
"A bit more practice and you'll
probably be fine."

Lexley vs. The Gravediggers

The trial was no bother at all. I couldn't stop scoring, so I got into the team straight away. Big Dan did his best but he swung and missed too much. Every time he did, the other kids jeered and he went red as a beetroot. Still, he never lost heart and when the others were all around me at the end, telling me I was brilliant, he was among them, panting like a big puppy, patting me on the back and gasping, "… 'tastic, mate! 'mazin'!" Dave told him he'd earned a place among the reserves.

Every game Lexley Under-10s played that season, Chrissie was there on the touchline, rain, sleet or shine. Mostly she jogged up and down with Dan who was always there, too, in his kit, gee-ing up the team. And if we were well on top, sometimes Dave would bring him

 on as a sub for ten minutes. When I asked him how come his mum and dad never turned up to support him, he

shrugged and said, "Workin'."

Just like mine then.

Chrissie never said much; not *Wow! You're getting really good.* That wasn't how she was. But she would quietly show me how to put a bit more bend on the ball from a corner kick, how to loop one up-and-over, trap a pass cleanly – all that kind of thing. "Position!" she would mutter if I was getting selfish or "Head up!" if I missed the best chance for a quick one-two. And she always had a word of praise for anything Dan got right. She spent ages showing him how to handle a ball that was coming fast along the ground from behind; and best of all, she showed him how to take one on his chest.

Dave thanked her for taking such an interest. "I'm surprised you never took up that Arsenal offer," he said. "You've really got it."

She shrugged. "Well … you know." He begged her to come and help on training nights. She looked doubtful. "You're wasted," he said.

The day of the Cup Final finally arrived. We were up against a team that boasted they had had been together since they were five and never lost an important match.

Cemetery Road, they were called. Alias The Gravediggers. They had a great goalie, a massive kid called Barnes with hands like shovels.

First half, all you could hear was COME ON YOU DIGGERS! It made you feel like *Woah! They really must be good.* Me and Mark Boxer had about eight shots on goal, all of which would have gone in normally but their goalie got a hand or a foot on everything we threw at him. Then I managed to dribble the ball past both the Diggers backs and into the penalty area. So it was just Barnsie, all spread out, and little old me. I made it look like I was going left and then … doof … nutmegged him. Sweet!

After that it was LEX-LEY! LEX-LEY! LEX-LEY!

Dave told us during half-time that he didn't think one-nil would be enough and he was worried because Mark, our main striker, was limping a bit. "Get warmed up, Warno," he said to Dan.

"Me?" said Dan, all shocked-looking, pointing to his chest. You could hear the rest of the team groaning and tutting.

Mark held out for five minutes in the second half, but he had slowed down too much to be much use and the Diggers drew level.

Dan was on the line with Chrissie when Dave signalled for him to go on. She helped him out of his track suit and held on to it for him and you could see her having a word, trying to get him to calm down and think about things. Meanwhile he was jumping up and down on the spot like a mad kangaroo.

For a good ten minutes, he was rubbish. Eric Slattery, our centre half, even shoved him off the ball to use it himself. That really got to me. "Oy, Slatts!" I yelled. "We're all in this together, you know!"

"Yeah. Sorry, mate," he said. Dan gave me a little wave of thanks, close to his chest, like.

Looking back, I can still see it in

my head in slow motion. The Diggers have all moved forward, desperate to get a winner. I take the ball right off the toe of their Number 9. I'm starting a run up the right wing. I'm so quick, I'm round one man, then another. None of our players can keep up. So I'm cutting into the box and Barnsie is there, like a big windmill, but I know I can easily draw him to me and slide one past him with my left.

Then I hear Dan, all wound up, shouting and going like a train out on the left, waving for a pass. I hear Slattery galloping behind me and moving to the right to draw the opposition. "On yer own!" he hisses. "Don't give it to him! He'll muff it!"

I take no notice. I check my run. The goalie is coming at me. I look up. "Yours, Danny!" I shout and put one up for him. It's high, but he's on to it. Oh, no, he's too fast! But then he leans back, dropping both arms and takes it on his chest just like Chrissie has shown him. The ball drops. One stride. Bang.

GOOOOOOOOOAAAAAAL!

The Long Arm of the Law

There's such a hullabaloo afterwards that I don't see my dad. But suddenly there he is, lifting me over his head and kissing me. Then he's hugging Chrissie and kissing her and saying "I'm sorry, I'm sorry. I've let you down. Both of you. But things are going to be different from

56

now on. I'm here now."

We're all in tears but we're all right. We've got each other now.

Somebody's tugging my sleeve. "He's here!" said Dan, all lit up. "He was on duty, but he managed to get away for the second half. Dad, meet my friend Jimmy Skinner. He's our star player."

"Yeah? What about your winner?" I say, grinning.

I suddenly realise that Dan's father is staring at me. Until then I haven't properly taken him in, except to notice he's bigger than my dad. When I take a proper look, I feel this wave of shock like a punch in the guts. I want the playing field to open and swallow me up. It's PC Beetroot!

"So this is your play-maker, is it?" he says, all cheery. Then, quick as a flash, his smile has gone. His eyes narrow and his round face begins to blaze like fire.

I am dead. I know it.

He goes on, serious now and having to shout to be heard over the noise of our supporters: "Well, he's got a wonderful turn of speed, hasn't he?" I can sense his policeman's mind ticking over.

Hearing him shout reminds me of the last thing I'd heard him yell as I legged it down the alley outside the mini-mart. *I've had a good look at you, sunshine! And I never forget a face!*

Sooner or later we're going to meet each other again. And then I'll have you! You hear me?"

I give my sister a look like a puppy stuck down a drain but I know that even she can't get me out of this mess. I lower my head and brace myself, waiting for the long arm of the law to come down hard on me at last.

The long arm stretched out all right, but with a friendly hand on the end of it. Instead of getting a tight grip on my collar, it gave me a couple of hearty thumps on the back.

"So *this* is the lad you've been telling me about, is it?" said Dan's dad, giving me a broad grin and a crunching hand-shake. "Dan's often told me how you've looked after him and what a good bloke you are."

What was going on? He knew I was a thief.

"I'm sorry we haven't had a chance to meet before," he said, giving me a steely look. "Great to meet you at last, Jimmy."

He can't have forgotten me, surely! Without taking his eyes off mine for a second, he continued: "I can see what Dan's been on about. Most kids would have gone for glory when the goal opened up like that. But when you crossed that ball for Dan … well! That was unselfish. That was proper old-fashioned, honest-to-goodness sportsmanship. Thank you. We owe you one, don't we, Daniel?"

Then he turned back to my dad and shook his hand. "You've got someone a bit special there, Mr Skinner."

"I know I have," said Dad. He put his arm round my shoulder. "I'm so proud of him. I only wish I could have been a bit better at showing it."

"Well, you're here now," I said quietly. "You and Chrissie. Thanks. And from now on, I'm going to do a lot more for you to be proud of."

Just to prove the point, I grabbed one handle of the Cup and pushed the other one towards Dan.

We hoisted that thing into the air and ran round the field with it together, screaming our heads off.

The End

… Well, nearly.

Just to add that the real hero –
sorry, heroine – of this story; in other
words, my sister Chrissie Skinner, is
now playing for Arsenal Ladies
Under-15s.

And only today she got a letter
offering her a trial for England!

As for Dad, he's behind us both,
all the way. And he's made sure that
Mum gets time off to come and

support us when we've got a big game on. Looking good, yeah?